McCordsville Elementary
Media Center

Quilt of Dreams

Mindy Dwyer

ALASKA NORTHWEST BOOKS™

"Snow!" yelled Katy, dropping her needle and thread. Running to the front door, she yanked it open and went out to dance with the snowflakes. "First snow!" she said, laughing and twirling as the tiny flakes kissed her upturned face.

Katy's family lived in the mountains where winter came early and stayed late. It was just Katy and Mom that winter. Dad had gone north to work, and Katy's grandma, who had lived with them, had died the summer before.

3

As the floating snow drifted into the house, Mom said, "Look at the snowflakes, Kate. No two are exactly alike."

Katy held a snowflake in her hand. It quickly melted and Katy sighed. "If Gram were here, she would celebrate the first snow with tea and sweets," she said.

Katy wanted to remember Gram for always. She closed her eyes and made a wish that her memories would never disappear like these beautiful snowflakes.

"Come inside Kate," Mom said with a shiver. "Let's get back to our sewing."

Winter was a time for sewing, and Mom and Katy were making a quilt.

Katy had been hard at work on her quilt since the day she had found Gram's sewing tin and scrap basket. Tucked neatly inside were colorful spools of thread, packets of shiny needles, and a little pair of elegant scissors shaped like a bird. Hidden among the colorful fabric scraps was a bundle of triangles labeled "Kate's Quilt." Only one quilt patch was complete—a square made of triangles.

"Gram must have started a quilt for you as a surprise!" Mom had said.

Katy wanted that quilt more than anything. "We can finish it together, can't we, Mom?" she'd asked.

Mom had hesitated. "Well, Gram was the quilter in the family . . . but let's try!"

Back inside the warm kitchen, Katy brushed the snowflakes from her hair and shoulders, then pulled one of Gram's old quilts off the couch and wrapped herself up in it. "Look, Mom!" she said. "There are little pictures sewn into the scraps of this quilt, and lots of crazy stitches hold the patches together."

"Isn't that pretty?" Mom said. "Gram used to say that quilts are bits and parts of special things you will never forget once they are made into something new. That's why no two quilts are exactly alike."

Katy traced Gram's work with her finger and whispered, "Yes. Like the snowflakes, no two are exactly alike."

8

"Is there something to remember in all of Gram's quilts?" Katy asked.

"Yes," Mom said, pointing to the quilt on Dad's chair. "Gram made that when your Dad and I first moved up to the mountains. The little red squares are the glow of the hearth, to keep us warm in our log cabin."

"And this one?" Katy touched the quilt folded over the back of the couch.

"That one is made from little squares of her grandchildren's clothes. See, this was your blouse," Mom said, smiling.

Katy's face lit up and her eyes sparkled. She said, "I wish I knew what was special about my quilt. I wonder why Gram cut out all those triangles?"

"I don't know," Mom said. "Maybe we'll find out as we put it together."

11

Every day after school, Katy worked on making neat, tiny stitches like Gram's. It was hard work and went slowly.

One day she became frustrated and threw down her quilt square, sighing, "I can't do it, Mom. My stitches are messy, and it takes too long."

Mom smoothed Katy's hair and said, "It does take a lot of time, but don't give up. I know you can do it. Gram used to say that quilts are made out of time."

Katy dug around in Gram's sewing tin and picked up the little bird scissors. Mom said, "Someday, when you've mastered your stitches, the scissors will be yours, okay?"

Katy thought they were the most beautiful scissors she had ever seen, and she wanted them for her very own. But how would she ever learn to sew like Gram? And what was this quilt going to look like?

13

One Saturday morning, as the long winter sunrise turned the snow shades of blue, Katy sat by the woodstove, trying to do her best. As she pulled the needle through the fabric, she poked her finger, and she blinked back tears.

Mom came over, kissed Katy's finger, and said, "When I was a little girl, I concentrated so hard on making my stitches nice and even like Gram's, do you know what happened? I sewed the fabric square right onto my skirt!

"Gram told me, 'Don't worry, honey. Mistakes can make things beautiful, too. Mistakes make them unique!' Then Gram sewed the square all around the edges to make a patch on my skirt. It was my favorite skirt after that."

Katy laughed, and the tears disappeared. "Let's sew some more, Mom. I'll keep trying."

The sun set early in winter afternoons, filling the room with alpenglow. As Mom sat down to quilt, the scissors reflected the pink of the setting sun, reminding Katy of Gram, who used to sit in the same rocker using the little scissors.

"Katy," Mom said. "I have something to tell you. Your Gram used these scissors for a long time. See, it's a little crane," Mom said as she swooshed the scissors through the air. "Gram loved birds, and the crane was her favorite. Do you know that cranes form families, and together they make the long journey north, year after year?"

"Every spring," Katy said.

"When people do something year after year, it's called tradition," Mom said. Katy traced the outline of the bird's wings.

"Mothers teach daughters what their mothers taught them, and it becomes very special through time," said Mom. "We are continuing a tradition by learning to quilt. Traditions are a gift from one generation to the next."

Katy smiled and wondered, Would she have a little girl herself one day? Would she teach her to sew?

17

The winter months surrounded
Katy and Mom with dark, snowy days.
Sewing kept their hands busy and
their hearts full of memories. One
night while they slept, a blizzard
brought so much snow that the next
morning school was cancelled!

"We still need more patches to finish the quilt, Katy," Mom said. Looking out the window, she shook her head. "With this storm it could be days before we get to town to buy more fabric." Katy searched through Gram's scrap basket to find pieces big enough to cut into triangle shapes. But then she got an idea. She ran upstairs to look for the dress Gram had made for her school picture day. It was too small for her now, so she brought the dress downstairs and began to cut it apart.

When Mom saw what she was doing, she chuckled. She left for a moment and returned, carrying some of Gram's old clothes. She said, "Let's be like the pioneer women. When they were snowed in, they would sew all the scraps they could find around the house into a blizzard quilt!"

All afternoon, the snow piled up in soft drifts. The woodstove crackled cheerfully as Mom and Katy stitched the new triangles. They took a break from sewing to bake cookies and celebrate the snow the way Gram used to, with a fresh pot of tea and warm, sweet treats.

As they sipped, Katy wondered again why Gram had chosen triangles for her quilt. "What do you think they're supposed to be, Mom? Are they mountains? Trees?"

Mom took a bite of her snickerdoodle and chewed thoughtfully. "It sure is a mystery, Kate," she said. "There must be some reason why she chose them for you."

That evening, with the warmth of the woodstove filling the room, Katy fell asleep on the couch with a quilt square still in her hand. Mom tiptoed around the finished patches on the floor and threw a quilt over Katy.

In the night, Katy saw her quilt squares moving around the room. With the magic found only in dreams, the fabric triangles rose up and began to flutter near the ceiling. Making strange sounds, the triangles became beautiful birds with magnificent wings. Then, gracefully they soared out the window and into a dark, snowy sky.

23

When Katy awoke, she shook her head—was she dreaming or did she really hear that sound?

She raced to the window and saw birds flying across the sky like arrows pointing north.

"Mom, look at the birds! It's a sign of spring! Dad will be home soon!"

Mom hurried in, tying her robe. "Oh, listen to the calls they make, Katy," she said. "They're cranes!"

The music of the cranes brought back a memory for both of them. When Katy was very young, she and Gram had watched hundreds of flying cranes, making that same sound. Once again, the cranes remembered the way north, as they had year after year.

"Katy, do you remember? After you and Gram saw the cranes, you dreamed about them for weeks," Mom said. "You would come downstairs, all sleepy-eyed, saying, 'I flew away last night!' You didn't know it was just a dream. You thought it was real. How Gram loved those mornings after you flew with the cranes!"

"I forgot all about that," Katy said.

24

After breakfast, Katy and Mom lined up all of their finished squares on the floor and looked at them. Katy suddenly realized that the triangles made a design of little arrows—just like the cranes she had seen flying across the sky that morning. "Mom, I think I've figured it out! These triangles look just like the shape the cranes make when they follow each other through the sky!"

"Katy, I think you're right!" said Mom.

They stared at the patches happily, seeing hundreds of cranes in them for the first time.

As she admired the colorful pattern, Katy noticed something. "Oops," she said, "that patch doesn't have triangles. Should we fix it?"

"No, let's not," Mom said. "I think the mistake looks beautiful there—and I even recognize the fabric. It's from your nightgown, your little flying nightgown!"

"Oh, wow!" said Katy, and she touched the patch. "Let's leave it just the way it is," she said.

26

27

Over the next few weeks, they joined the squares together to make the top of the quilt. They used Gram's curtains to make a bottom layer. And between the top and bottom, they put soft cotton filling for warmth, and made thousands of tiny quilting stitches to hold all three layers together.

Looking at the rows of stitches, Katy said, "They look like little footsteps walking down a path."

"A path of memories," said Mom. "Just as these stitches hold the quilt together, our sewing connects us, you and Gram and me," she continued. "Gram would be proud."

Mom held out her hand. There, tied with a ribbon like soft tail feathers, were Gram's crane scissors for Katy.

Katy blushed with joy.

On the glorious night the quilt was finished, Mom tucked Katy into bed and whispered, "There's an old saying. *Sleep under a new quilt and your dreams will come true.*"

Katy couldn't stop smiling. She felt part of something—part of a tradition. Gram had started her quilt of dreams, and Katy and Mom had finished it. As she grew older, Katy would look at her quilt and remember Gram always.

As Katy slept, tiny snowflakes sparkled, no two exactly alike. Cranes soared across the sky, and in her dream, Katy followed. Looking back, she thought she saw Gram in the window, smiling and waving.

For my mother, Audrey, and for
her mother, Gladys—my grandma.

—M. D.

Text and illustrations © 2000 by Mindy Dwyer
Book compilation © 2000 by Alaska Northwest Books™
An imprint of Graphic Arts Center Publishing Company
P.O. Box 10306, Portland, Oregon 97296-0306, 503-226-2402; www.gacpc.com

Library of Congress Cataloging-in-Publication Data

Dwyer, Mindy, 1957–
    Quilt of dreams / text and illustrations by Mindy Dwyer.
        p.   cm.
    Summary: While working on a quilt that her grandmother had
started before she died, Katy discovers the special memories
and meanings that are part of every quilt.
        ISBN 0-88240-522-5 (hbd.)
        ISBN 0-88240-521-7 (sbd.)
        [1. Quilts—Fiction.   2. Grandmothers—Fiction.]   I. Title.
PZ7.D9635 Qu 2000
[E]—dc21
                                                                00-036270
                                                                CIP

President: Charles M. Hopkins
Editorial Staff: Douglas A. Pfeiffer, Timothy W. Frew, Ellen Harkins Wheat,
    Tricia Brown, Jean Andrews, Alicia I. Paulson
Production Staff: Richard L. Owsiany, Susan Dupere
Designer: Elizabeth Watson

Printed on acid- and chlorine-free paper in Singapore

Author's Note

Gram's "gift of the generations" is tradition, a handing down of customs that helps keep culture alive. Imagine stitching the very same pattern that pioneer women might have pieced by the light of a candle or in the back of a wagon.

The pioneer ethic stressed the use of every scrap of fabric (perhaps the beginning of recycling), and buying new fabric was the last resort. Even quilt patterns are reused year after year, although every quilter sews her own family's stories into her quilt, making each unique.

The traditional quilt patterns you see or read about in this book include these old American quilt designs.

Birds in the Air (pages 26, 27, 28, 29, cover, endsheets): Birds in the Air is one of the many patterns derived from nature. The rows of triangles were thought to resemble birds flying overhead. This pattern is one of the earliest nineteenth-century American patterns that were based on the simple organization of triangles. More complex variations grew as the design passed from quilter to quilter and region to region.

Blizzard Quilt (page 15): When a blizzard was coming, pioneer women quickly sewed "blizzard quilts" out of scraps around the house, and sometimes stuffed them with old, worn quilts to keep their families warm.

Crazy Quilt (pages 2, 9, 22): Crazy quilts were the first quilts to serve as decorative household furnishings instead of functional bed coverings. There was great satisfaction in using up scraps of irregular shapes, but more importantly, quilting was one of the few outlets available for pioneer women to express themselves artistically.

Grandma's Square (page 11): One of the most interesting aspects of quilt lore lies in the names given to the patterns. Often called "folklore's poetry," the names show true imagination. Sometimes the same patterns were known by different names in different regions. Variations of Grandma's Square are also called Trip Around the World, Sunshine and Shadow, and Grandma's Dream.

Log Cabin (page 10): The Log Cabin design has remained popular for more than a century. Nearly every cultural group and generation has made the pattern, contributing their own unique design elements along the way. Each block is created with concentric strips, or "logs," around a central patch. This center patch is often red to symbolize the cabin's hearth fire.